D1489031

Library of Congress Cataloging in Publication Data

White, Wallace, 1930-
The storm.

(A Triumph book)
Summary: Sixteen-year-old Mike, suspected of
setting a fire at a marina, survives a storm at sea
and learns to accept responsibility for his own life.
[1. Boats and boating—Fiction] I. Title.
PZ7.W5848ST   [Fic]   82-4852
SBN 0-531-04425-4   AACR2

R. L. Spache Revised Formula 2.4

THE STORM

BY PETER NYE

Franklin Watts
New York / London / Toronto / Sydney / 1982
A Triumph Book

"We ought to fix old man Crane," said Gary. He looked angry.

"Right," said Mike. He felt angry himself. None of the young people in Galway Bay liked Mr. Crane. Mainly, that was because Mr. Crane didn't seem to like young people.

Mike and Gary were standing on a slope not far from a little white building. The building was the marina office. And beyond the office was the marina itself—a large boat basin with still blue water. About fifty motorboats and sailboats were tied up there. Mr. Crane was in charge of the marina. Lately, he had been giving Mike and some of his friends a bad time.

Mike said, "We could go talk to Crane—we could tell him what we think of him."

Gary frowned. "Let's think of something better."

"Like what?"

"I don't know. Something really big."

Mike shrugged. He felt confused. He and Gary both wanted to do something to hurt Mr. Crane. But if they were going to teach Mr. Crane a lesson, Mike thought, they should do it right.

Just yesterday, Mr. Crane had told Mike and his friends to stay away from the marina. That was because they had taken a radio down to the docks after school. They played the radio as loud as they could. Mr. Crane said they were hoodlums. He shouted at them to leave. Finally they did. But Mr. Crane had no right to talk to them like that. Galway Bay was their town, too. And the marina was part of the town. Mike had spent all sixteen of his years here. It was one of the best towns in Florida, with good weather most of the year. And it was great for sailing. As soon as Mike had a job, and some money, he wanted to get a boat of his own.

"I've got an idea," said Gary. He pointed to the office. "See that model ship?"

The office had a glassed-in porch. And on the porch, on a table, was a model of a full-rigged ship. It was about three feet long and nearly as high. It was a beauty.

Mike said, "What about it?"

"Let's take it."

"Take it?"

"Rip it off," said Gary. "Crane built it himself. If we take it, he'll go nuts."

"What will we do with it?"

"Who cares?" Gary said. He pulled out a cig-arette and lit it.

"Yeah, but what if Crane comes?"

"He's not around," Gary said. "His car's not in the parking lot. See?"

Mike glanced at the lot, near the office. Gary was right. "Yeah, but what if . . ." He didn't finish his question, though. He was thinking. Gary had been a friend of Mike's since elementary school. Gary was a wiry, athletic boy with a good sense of humor. Over the years, they had had a lot of fun together. They had got into a little trouble together, too. But Mike didn't know whether stealing the model ship made much sense. Would Mr. Crane understand what had happened?

Suddenly a tall, bearded young man rounded the corner. He was carrying a cardboard carton. He walked toward Mike and Gary saying, "What are you punks up to?"

The bearded guy was named Joe Easton, but most people called him Tiger Joe. He was about twenty-two, and he was thin, with a long face and pale blue eyes. On his left arm was a tattoo of a tiger. Of all the people around the harbor, Tiger Joe was probably the strangest. Joe didn't come from Galway Bay. He had been born in Iowa. Six or seven years ago he had dropped out of school. Then he had drifted around for several years.

About a year ago, Tiger Joe Easton had turned up here in Galway Bay. He had an old thirty-foot cruiser, the *Tiger Lily*. And he rented a space for his boat at the marina. Ever since, he had been living there on his boat. He never seemed to do any work, but he always seemed to get by. Sometimes you could hear Tiger Joe playing an old harmonica. He would sit on the deck of his boat and play—a clear, reedy sound. The music would drift up and down the docks.

Mike had always liked Tiger Joe. He was older than most of Mike's friends. He was more experienced. And there was something about Joe that was sort of fascinating. Joe could talk about all kinds of things—about other places, other towns, books, music, girls. He seemed kind of free. Joe seemed to know a great deal about the world, and, in a way Mike could not explain, there was something mysterious about him.

Once, Mike had spent a whole day on Tiger Joe's boat, helping him work on some equipment. Joe had talked to him about how to get along with people. "First thing is, you've got to remember everybody's got their own scene going," Joe had said. "Too many people, they—well, they don't understand that. *I* didn't used to. Anyway, think about where *they're* at. People always see you through their own eyes—know what I mean?"

Mike said, "Yeah, I guess."

"You've got a lot going for you," Tiger Joe said then. "You're young. You're smart. Don't foul things up."

Mike hadn't been exactly sure what Joe meant by that. But he had not forgotten it. Now Mike said, "What's happening, Joe?"

"I've just been picking up some supplies," Tiger Joe said. "You punks look like you're up to no good."

Gary exhaled smoke. He said, "It's just—we thought we'd fix old man Crane. See that model ship? We thought we'd rip it off."

Tiger Joe looked toward the office. "You kids are nuts," he said. "I'll see you around."

"Hey, Joe . . . " Mike began. But Tiger Joe swung around and set off toward the other end of the marina, where his boat was docked.

Mike and Gary watched Tiger Joe walk down the deck. Joe always walked with a slight limp. He never talked about what was wrong with his leg. But some people said he had got in trouble somewhere overseas, that he had been injured in some sort of fight.

Gary said, "How about it, Mike?"

Mike was thinking. Tiger Joe said he didn't like the idea of stealing the ship. Still, they ought to do *something* to Mr. Crane. Finally he said, "O.K. . . . I guess . . . Let's do it."

The two boys walked quickly down the hill to the office. The door was unlocked. They opened it and stepped onto the porch. Mike noticed a strong smell. He glanced around and realized that Mr. Crane must have just painted the porch.

Gary put his hands on the three-masted model ship. He said, "O.K. You take. . . ." He hesitated. "Wait a minute—hey. . . ." He was trying to lift the ship. But it wouldn't move. Gary scowled and said, "He's got it *nailed down*."

"Huh?" Mike was at the other end of the little ship. He grasped it, tried to lift it. Gary was right. In some way—with nails or glue—Mr. Crane had fastened the model ship to the table. "Maybe we ought to forget it," he said.

"No, wait," said Gary. "I've got an idea."

"What?"

Gary held out his cigarette. "See?" he said with a grin.

"Wait a minute. . . ."

"Watch," Gary said. Reaching out with his cigarette, he touched it to one of the cloth sails. After a few seconds, a small, yellowish flame appeared. It began to climb up the sail.

Mike gasped. "Gary!" He grabbed his friend's arm. "Hey! What are you doing?"

The yellow flame had jumped to another sail, and another.

"What are you *doing*?" said Mike. "It's *spreading*!"

Gary muttered, "We'd better get out of here."

"Yeah, but. . . ." Mike glanced through the glass of the porch. He saw a man walking along the dock. "Somebody's coming!"

"Who?"

"I don't know!"

"Let's split," said Gary.

The two of them stumbled out the door, back onto the dock.

Gary glanced at the man on the dock. He said, "It's the guard. I'll see you later." He started running back up the slope.

Mike stood there. He looked at the office. The model ship was already a mass of flames. The flames were climbing toward the roof. Then, suddenly, they leapt to the wall of the porch. The fresh paint had caught fire. A sheet of flame started racing up the wall.

Mike couldn't believe his eyes. But for some reason, he couldn't seem to move. He knew he should act. Instead, he just stood there, watching, as the flames licked the walls of the little building. It was as if he should do something. But what?

He caught his breath. The man, the marina's guard, was only about fifty feet away now. And he had begun to trot toward the office.

At last Mike turned. He wasn't sure whether the guard recognized him or not. He began to run.

There was a firebox about a block away. Mike

ran up the slope toward it. He turned and looked behind him. The entire front of the office was on fire. He broke the glass of the firebox and pulled the alarm.

He didn't wait for the fire trucks to come, though. Instead, he started for home, running most of the way. Mike lived about a half mile from there. All the way, as he ran, he thought about what he and Gary had just done. A fire! Things had gone all wrong. Why had Mike ever let himself be talked into such a dumb thing?

About five minutes later, Mike was home. He was out of breath. And he felt frightened and nervous and guilty. As he walked in, he heard his mother's voice say, "Is that you, Michael?"

"Yeah," Mike said.

"It's nearly five thirty." His mother came into the living room. She was a soft-looking woman with kind eyes. Alice Denton was a good housekeeper and an excellent cook, and in her spare time she sometimes painted watercolors, mostly of landscapes around Galway Bay. She said, "Where have you been?"

"I was down at the marina," Mike said, trying

to sound casual. "We were . . . messing around."

She gave him a penetrating look. Mike wondered if, maybe, she could see right through him, could guess what he and Gary had been up to.

Alice Denton said, "Your father wants you to move those old suitcases into the spare room."

"Oh yeah? O.K., I'll do it after dinner," said Mike. He had other things on his mind now. He walked through the hall and opened the door of his room. He went in and closed the door.

Alone, he sat down on his bed. In his mind, he could see the model ship, bursting into flames. It wasn't the first time Mike had gotten into a mess, and sometimes he just thought he had no will of his own. He sat there and stared at the wall. Then he got up and put a record on his stereo. He turned the volume up. But as the record played, he realized he wasn't really listening.

After about a half hour, he heard a car pull up in the driveway. He knew his father had come home. Lou Denton was a big man with strong arms and a beefy face. He worked in a garage, and the first thing he always did when he came home was to shower, to get some of the grease off. Mike loved his father, but he didn't want to grow up to be like him. Lou Denton always had a list of rules for everything. If Mike was late for dinner, the rule was that Mike had to wash dishes. If Mike came in later than ten thirty on a weeknight, the rule was that he couldn't go out for the next two nights. About four years ago, Mr. Denton even developed a progress chart for Mike. It was made out each week and it showed Mike's good points and bad points. Mike didn't like the idea at all. He didn't think everything in life should depend on rules and charts.

Now Mike could hear the shower running. He could hear his parents talking. At about six thirty, his mother called him for dinner. Mike went into the kitchen and sat down with his parents at the table.

During dinner, Mike felt miserable. He couldn't think of anything but the model ship, the office, the fire. And when his mother or his father asked him questions—about school or his friends—he was barely able to answer.

Lou Denton sat there eating hamburger steak. Suddenly, he looked up at Mike. He said, "What's the trouble? You're not eating."

"I guess I'm not hungry," said Mike.

"You need your food," his father said. "You'll need it if you're going to go out for baseball this spring. Right?"

"Yeah, I guess," said Mike. Last year, Mike had played in the outfield on the school team. He was pretty good.

The phone rang.

Mr. Denton got up to answer it. The phone was in the hall. From the kitchen, Mike could hear his father's voice.

After a few minutes, Lou Denton came back into the kitchen. His face looked strained.

Alice Denton looked up. "What's the matter?"

"The matter? The *matter?*" Lou Denton said.

"That was Mr. Crane, down at the marina. He told me some boys set fire to the office building this afternoon. The guard saw them. And one of the boys . . ." he turned toward Mike, ". . . one of them looked like *you*."

Mike winced.

His father said, "Were you part of it, Mike? Were you down there?"

Mike gripped his leg under the table. Should he lie, or should he tell his parents the truth? He hated to lie. But if he told them everything, he was afraid his father might punish him—might even go back to whipping him with a strap. And Lou Denton hadn't done that for years.

"Mike—answer me!" Mr. Denton said.

Finally Mike said, "Look . . . I was in on it. I mean . . . I mean, it was a stupid idea. We never meant it to go so far. It was just supposed to be a joke."

"A joke!" Lou Denton said. "Some joke! You go set a building on fire!"

"Yeah, but we. . . ."

His father looked as if he were about to explode. He said, "I'm going to give you two choices. Either you go to Mr. Crane and tell him exactly what you did—I mean *everything.* Or else I'm going to go talk to the police—before Mr. Crane does. I'll go tell them who was responsible for that fire!"

Mike couldn't believe what his father had said. It was as if he were on the other side, before he even knew Mike's side of the story. Mike said, "It wasn't as bad as it sounds. We just—we were just going to have some fun. . . ."

"I've had about enough of your kind of fun!" Mr. Denton shouted. "Who else was in on it, anyway? Who was the other boy?"

Mike was silent.

Alice Denton signaled to her husband to calm down.

But by this time Mike couldn't take any more. He said, "Excuse me, please," and he got up hurriedly and left the table. He left the room, but he barely knew where he was going. Behind him, he could hear his father's voice, telling him to come back.

Mike didn't go back to the kitchen, though. He headed for his room. In the hall was a watercolor Alice Denton had done—an old lighthouse just north of town. Not far from it was Mike's chart, hanging on the wall between the bathroom and Mike's room. Mike hated to look at the thing. It had a space for each day of the week. If Mike did something right, he got a gold star. If he did something wrong, he got a blue circle. At the end of each week, the gold stars and the blue circles were added up. If there were more stars, he had a good week. Then his father put some money—the same amount as Mike's allowance—into a special bank account for Mike. But if there were more circles, Mike had a bad week, and he was assigned extra chores around the house.

This week, so far, Mike had received one gold star and three blue circles. Mike always felt embarrassed when his friends came over and saw the chart. He didn't know any other kids who had anything like that.

Mike went into his room and closed the door. Should he go to Mr. Crane, as his father insisted, and tell him what he and Gary had done? What should he do?

If he kept silent, he knew that things would get worse and worse.

He threw himself on his bed and tried to think.

The next morning was like torture. At breakfast, Lou Denton told Mike again that he would have to go talk to Mr. Crane. And in school, all Mike could think of was the fire. At about ten, he ran into Gary in the hall.

"Listen," Gary whispered. "Old man Crane's talking about going to the D.A.—"

"The district attorney!" Mike caught his breath. "How do you know?"

"I heard some kids talking about it. Just now. You know Pete Vargas? His brother does some work for Crane. They say the guard recognized you. They say setting a fire is arson. That's a crime. And Crane says he's going to go to the cops and everything."

"Are you sure?"

"I'm not *sure*. But that's what Pete says. How come you didn't run faster, Mike? How come you didn't split when I did?"

Mike didn't know what to say. This just made everything worse.

The bell rang, and they went to their classes. During geometry, Mike kept thinking of what Gary had just said. And when the bell rang again, at eleven, he knew he had to do something—something to get him out of this mess.

He left school. He walked fast, and within fifteen minutes he was at the marina. The office looked very bad. Mike hurried past the damaged building, and luckily, he didn't see Mr. Crane. He kept walking down the main dock. There was one person who might understand, who might have some ideas—Tiger Joe.

The *Tiger Lily* was tied up at the end of the dock. Its hull was white, but the boat looked kind of battered. More than once, Mr. Crane had called the *Tiger Lily* an eyesore. Mike was pretty sure the boat was seaworthy, though. Joe often worked on the engine. Recently, he had bought a new bilge pump. And on board there was a good life preserver.

Before Mike reached the boat, he knew Joe was aboard. He could hear Joe's harmonica. Joe was playing an old song. Mike didn't know its name, but it sounded kind of mournful. When Mike reached the boat, he found Tiger Joe sitting near the stern, in the sunshine. Joe was wearing a floppy old hat, looking toward the sea.

"Joe!" Mike called. "Hey, Joe . . . I want to come aboard."

The music stopped. Joe turned and said, "Huh? O.K. What's up?"

Mike climbed aboard. Then he stood on the deck and told Joe everything that had happened.

Tiger Joe gave him a clouded look. He said, "You kids really *are* nuts. I didn't think you'd go that far."

"Yeah, but the thing is, what do I do *now?*"

"Are you going to get Gary involved?" Joe asked.

Mike swallowed. "No, I'm not going to say anything about Gary. What Crane doesn't know won't hurt him."

"What are you going to do, then?"

"I don't know. I mean . . . I thought maybe you'd have some ideas."

Joe shook his head. He said softly, "I can't tell you what to do, Mike. Some things you've just got to figure out in your own head."

Mike looked at the gentle waves beyond the boat's gunwales. Finally, almost not daring to hope, he said, "Hey, Joe, listen. Things are really getting bad here. I'm thinking maybe I should . . . maybe I should ship out or something. I mean, I saw you stocking up on supplies. Are you going to sail pretty soon? Because I. . . ."

Tiger Joe frowned. "I figured I'd head down toward the Keys. Tomorrow morning, probably. But. . . ."

"Well. . . . Do you think I could. . . ."

"Forget it," said Joe.

"Wait a minute, Joe," Mike said. "Look, if you would take me along. . . ."

Tiger Joe shook his head. "I always sail alone. You know that." Then he squinted at the sun. He said, "I wish I could help you, man. But I can't think of a thing right now."

"Joe . . . Joe, listen . . . I'm scared. . . ."

Joe said something odd then. Shading his eyes, he said, "Everybody's scared, pal. Everybody *I* ever knew." He looked away again, toward the sea.

"Yeah, but. . . ." Mike stood there speechless. He had thought that Joe would offer to help him, somehow.

But Joe just sat there with a strange, thoughtful

look on his face. Then, suddenly, he looked up at Mike. He said, "Listen, I'm sorry you're in trouble, Mike." He reached into his pocket, fumbled around, and pulled out something. He shoved it into Mike's hand.

"What . . ." said Mike.

"Take it," said Tiger Joe.

Mike looked down at his hand. It was the harmonica. Mike said, "Joe . . . this is yours."

"No it isn't. I just gave it to you."

"But. . . ."

"I got it a long time ago, in Belgrade, Yugoslavia—got it from a street salesman," Joe said. He looked at Mike solemnly, saying, "The guy told me that if you have heart, the thing plays all by itself."

"If . . . what?" Mike was bewildered. *"If you have heart. . . .* What is *that* supposed to mean?"

"How should I know?" Tiger Joe said.

Mike stood there looking at Tiger Joe's sunburned face. He put the harmonica in his pocket. He felt grateful for the gift, but he was confused.

How was *this* going to help him out of his troubles? He didn't even know how to play the harmonica.

He turned and stepped off the *Tiger Lily*. From far out at sea came the sound of a ship's horn.

When his father came home from work that evening, Mike tried to talk to him again. But he soon realized it was hopeless. They were in the living room. Lou Denton asked Mike whether he had gone to talk to Mr. Crane yet.

"Not yet," said Mike. "I just couldn't. I mean, I've been thinking about the whole thing. . . ."

His father frowned. "I told you you had to do something today."

"I know. But it's not easy, Dad. Really. I've got to think."

"About what?"

"About what I'm going to say."

Lou Denton sucked in his breath. "You just say the truth! That's all you say! Go to Crane and tell him what you did!"

His father just didn't seem to understand. Why was it, when Mike needed help, his father just turned against him? Mike said, "I figured. . . ."

"I never thought you'd make me ashamed of you—not like this," Mr. Denton said. "I'm *ashamed.*"

"Please, Dad. . . ."

"Do you realize . . ." his father went on. "When I was your age, we used to have some respect for people—respect for property." He shoved his hands into his pockets. He shook his head, saying, "Sometimes I just don't know whether I'm doing the right thing with you. . . . I just don't know. . . . All right, I'll give you till tomorrow morning. But that's all!"

That night in bed Mike tossed and turned. All sorts of things went through his mind. The fire. Mr. Crane. Other problems—smaller ones—that Mike had been having at home with his parents. And then Mike remembered the harmonica. Why on earth had Tiger Joe given it to him?

Obviously, Joe had wanted to show Mike that he liked him. But at the same time, Joe refused to help him. Why? What harm would it do if Joe let Mike come along when he sailed tomorrow morning? Because Mike was getting fed up with everything now—Mr. Crane, the cops, the district attorney. And if Mr. Crane was going to cause all kinds of trouble for Mike, why should Mike stay here at all? Why shouldn't he get out of Galway Bay? Right now, before things got worse. Even Mike's father seemed to be against him—and that hurt Mike a lot. So why shouldn't he leave home and start a new life—the way Tiger Joe had done.

Mike thought of some things that Joe had told him about himself. After he left home in Iowa, Joe said that he had traveled to Africa. He had traveled to Greece and Turkey and other countries, too. He even said that he had met some famous people. Mike didn't believe everything Joe said—some of it sounded pretty fantastic. Still, the way Joe talked, being on your own—independent and free— sounded pretty great.

And then, for some reason, Mike felt funny. Because he remembered something his father had said a long time ago. One day, his father had begun talking about the man he worked for at the garage. Lou Denton had had a big argument with his boss. Things had finally worked out O.K., but Lou Denton had told Mike, "See? One of the most important things in life is to be straight with people. Don't try to get at people behind their backs. If you have a problem, take it right to the person involved."

"Is that being straight?" Mike had asked.

"It's part of it," Lou Denton had said. "A lot of people nowadays, they forget some of the simplest things. Understand what I mean?"

"Sort of," said Mike.

"But there are rules in life," Lou Denton went

on. "There are rules that took people centuries and centuries to learn. They tell you how to get along with other people all your life, and with yourself."

But Mike wasn't so sure. Because sometimes he couldn't see any rules at all. And anyway, he thought, what good were a bunch of rules when you were frightened and confused? Sometimes, he thought, you just had to go by a voice inside.

And now—as if he could hear a voice deep inside—Mike knew he had to act. And he also knew that he didn't have any time to waste.

He got out of bed. He dressed quickly. Then he glanced around the room. The harmonica was lying on top of his dresser. Should he take it? He picked it up and slipped it into his pocket. He tiptoed out of his room and walked down the hall. He opened the front door. He was outside. He started walking down the street.

The sea had always attracted Mike anyway. All his life he had dreamed of being on the open ocean, free. . . .

It was after midnight when Mike reached the *Tiger Lily*. He was surprised to see lights below-decks.

He stood on the deck, calling softly, "Joe!"

At first there was no answer. Mike called the name several times before Joe's head appeared at the top of the companionway.

Joe looked bleary-eyed. "What are you doing here?"

"Joe . . . I'm going with you."

Joe shook his head. "No way."

"But I've *got* to, Joe."

Tiger Joe stepped on deck. He stood with his hand on the railing. "I told you this afternoon—I can't help you, man. Anyway, I wish you wouldn't do this to me. . . . I'm not really good for you. . . . I've told you before."

It was true. Before now, Tiger Joe had told Mike not to hang out with him so much. Mike never understood. He said, "I'm only asking for a ride."

Tiger Joe looked annoyed. He met Mike's eyes. He said, "Better go back home, Mike. Look— I'll try to think of something. If I think of something, I'll let you know."

"How can you let me know? You'll be gone!"

"O.K., O.K. I'm sorry I can't help you, Mike. Take care, huh? I'm really sorry about all this." He frowned. He bit his lip. Then he turned and disappeared down the companionway.

Far out over the ocean, the moon had risen. It was a great yellow disc. It cast its glow over the black water.

Mike stood looking at the rippling water, the soft waves. He couldn't let things end this way. Anyway, he knew a lot about boats. From the time he was six or seven, he had hung around the marina. The summer when he was eleven he had helped out on a fishing boat. He had learned a lot. He really felt as if he knew almost enough to captain a vessel himself.

He stepped back onto the dock. Then he moved off slowly and sat down cross-legged near a wooden piling.

He waited nearly an hour, till the lights on the *Tiger Lily* went out. He waited nearly a half hour more. Then he approached the cruiser again. He stepped back onto its deck. Aft, behind the cockpit, was a large settee. Underneath the settee, there was storage space. Tiger Joe had thrown a tarpaulin over the settee. There, under the tarp—that's where Mike would hide.

He slipped under the tarp, a stowaway.

Time dragged by.

Mike thought morning would never come. His left arm was getting cramped. Lying underneath the tarpaulin, on the damp deck, he felt like a trapped animal. For a while, his thoughts seemed jumbled. He found himself thinking about all his problems, and especially Tiger Joe's refusal to help him. But then his thoughts began to drift. He fell asleep.

He was awakened by the sound of feet.

He remembered where he was. The smell of the dirty tarpaulin was strong in his nostrils. Joe had come up from the cabin. Mike could see daylight. He lay there listening as Joe walked around. He could hear Joe go back down the companionway. He heard Joe come up again. Finally Mike heard the *Tiger Lily's* diesel engine starting up.

Mike knew that he still had a good time to wait. It was another five minutes before he heard Tiger Joe walking around again. He heard a couple of thuds. He knew that Joe had cast off. He felt the boat begin to move.

He decided to wait a while longer. He knew he had to stay hidden until they were well out to sea. The wait seemed endless. He wondered what Joe would say when he saw him. And as his thoughts drifted, he remembered an afternoon months ago. Mike and Joe had been strolling near the town's amusement arcade. And Joe had begun to talk about his own childhood. He had a brother, Joe said, but he and his brother never got along. "Maybe that's one reason I left home," Joe said. "I'm not really sure. But see, it was like my folks always treated him different than me. I mean, he's a real bright guy—two years older than me—and he always got good grades. I was always fouling up. So one day, Ted came home and told us he'd won a scholarship to the university. And by that time—I hate to tell you, pal—by that time, I was in a little trouble with the law. Everybody thought Ted was the greatest—but it was like they were ashamed of me. So one day, I just cut out. Split. I've never seen my family since. They know where I am, more or less. But for me, that's all in the past." Joe smiled and added, "That's the sad story of Tiger Joe."

Now Mike blinked. Slowly, he crawled from under the tarp. "Joe. . . ."

Joe whirled from the helm. "*You!* What are you doing on board?"

"I couldn't understand why you wouldn't let me come, Joe. I thought. . . ."

Tiger Joe scowled. "Listen—you may not believe this—but I was trying to do you a favor. You don't belong out here!"

"All I want is a *ride*, Joe. I'll go ashore at the next port. I swear."

Joe frowned, looking out at the water. Mike looked at the water, too. They were at least ten miles from shore now. And the sky was beginning to grow cloudy. From the east, the sea seemed to be rising. A fog had begun to drift around the boat. The *Tiger Lily* had begun to toss and roll on the waves.

Joe turned back to Mike. His voice sounded harsh. "Why did you have to go and do this? Didn't you hear what I said yesterday afternoon?"

Mike watched Tiger Joe begin to limp toward the companionway. Suddenly Joe slipped and nearly fell. He steadied himself by grabbing a rail. Then, as if he had changed his mind about something, Joe went back to the wheel. The waves were growing surprisingly high. And over the past fifteen minutes, the sky had grown much darker. Mike felt sure that a storm was gathering. But how could this have happened so quickly?

"Listen, Joe," Mike said. "It looks like rough weather. I can help. I can spell you at the wheel."

Tiger Joe didn't answer. Instead, he steered the boat a bit to starboard and slowed to three or four knots.

For the next half hour, Tiger Joe stood at the wheel. And most of the time neither he nor Mike spoke. Then, suddenly, as the waves grew higher, Tiger Joe cut the engine.

"Why are we stopping, Joe?" Mike asked.

"Got some business . . ." Joe murmured. "Now listen to me—this is important. You've got to keep down. Way down. Stay out of sight."

Mike didn't ask why. He crouched near the tarpaulin. He didn't understand any of this. Then, like a ghostly presence in a dream, a shadowy shape appeared. It was another boat. It was approaching the *Tiger Lily*. In the fog, Mike could see the outlines of a little trawler.

"What . . ." Mike began.

But Tiger Joe wheeled around. "Shhh!" he said. "Keep down, Mike. Stay still!"

Mike did as he was told. He pulled part of the tarpaulin over him. Water had begun to slosh over the gunwales. Sea spray cut across his face. The other boat had pulled in very close, and Mike could see some figures on its deck. Both boats were being tossed about by the waves. Two men on the other boat were moving toward the *Tiger Lily*.

Mike peered up from the edge of the tarp. He couldn't make out the men's faces, but he saw Tiger Joe give them something. Then he saw one of the men hand Joe a shiny object. Tiger Joe took the object and muttered something. Mike couldn't understand any words. The wind was high.

Joe placed the shiny object to the port side of the helm. The object seemed to be a large can of some sort. The men exchanged a few more words. Then the trawler's engine revved up, and the trawler moved off into the fog.

Tiger Joe stepped back to the wheel. And the *Tiger Lily* was moving again, away from the vanishing shape of the other boat.

Now Mike knew that something was really wrong. He crawled out from under the tarp. What was this all about? One thing was clear—whatever was happening, it wasn't exactly ordinary. Boats don't usually approach each other silently in the fog. And things aren't usually passed secretly from one boat to another. Mike wasn't stupid. He felt sure that whatever had happened, it must be illegal.

The can was only a few feet away from Mike. It shone dully in the pale light. But he didn't dare go over to it. Not yet. The boat was beginning to roll in higher and higher waves.

Somehow, he had to think of a way to handle all this. But now Tiger Joe seemed to be having trouble. Joe turned and shouted, "Mike—come here! Take the wheel a minute! Hurry up, Mike! There's a knock in the engine. I can hear it!"

Mike had heard it, too, a thudding sound, as soon as Joe had started the engine again. He had to think fast. He would do what Tiger Joe asked—at least for now. If the boat's safety was involved, he would help. Stumbling, almost falling, Mike moved up to the helm. He took the wheel from Tiger Joe. The bow of the *Tiger Lily* plunged into a valley between waves, and Mike felt himself being thrown forward. He clung tightly to the wheel.

Once, he glanced around. Behind him, Tiger Joe had pulled up the engine hatch. Joe was shining a flashlight into the dark space beneath the deck. Water was continuing to pour over the sides of the boat. Mike could feel water around his ankles. He was doing his best to keep the boat on an even keel, but the rough sea seemed to be trying to yank it from his grasp. He felt his muscles straining.

Joe was still fumbling around near the engine. The wind howled. It was several minutes before Mike heard Joe close the hatch.

"We've got a problem, but I can't do anything about it now," Tiger Joe said. Then he muttered, "I should have checked the engine out yesterday—what's the matter with me?"

But Mike had to follow this thing through. Wasn't he involved now, too? Feeling his shoulders tighten, he said, "Joe, what's in that can? What's this all about?"

There was a bright flash of light. A few seconds later, there was a clap of thunder. Rain began to pour down in silvery sheets.

"I didn't expect this storm," Tiger Joe said, his

voice raw. "The reports didn't say anything about it—just winds. It's a freak—it's a freak storm! I've never seen one come up like this!"

"Joe . . . what's in that can?"

Tiger Joe was standing by his side now. With strong hands, he grasped the wheel and took it from Mike. "Better get back there," Joe said. "Stay aft, Mike. Keep your eyes out for lights. We may need help."

Water was sloshing around Mike's feet. Water was running down his face. But he was determined to find out everything now. He would keep a look-out, as Tiger Joe said. But first he had to find out the truth. He made his way over to the can. He knelt down on the deck. With his fingers, he tried to pry off the can's lid. It was tightly sealed. His fingers slipped. He dug his nails under the lid.

"Mike . . . get your hands off that thing!" Joe yelled.

The boat lurched upward, hovered on the crest of a wave, and crashed down into a gray-green valley.

Mike stood up. "Tell me what it is, then! What's in the can?"

"Nothing—nothing—nothing!" Joe yelled.

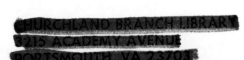

"Get away from that thing, Mike! Stay cool!"

"I *am* cool!" Mike yelled back. "Tell me what it is—I'm warning you!" Mike was surprised to hear his own words. Warning—warning Joe of what?

Joe was shouting, "It's sugar . . . it's nothing!"

But now—as if Joe had told him everything—Mike suddenly realized what was in the can. It was like a burst of knowledge. And now he knew, more or less, what had gone on between Joe and the men on the trawler. A transaction. A sale. The words caught in Mike's throat as he said, "Is it dope, Joe? Is that what it is?"

"Keep your eyes on the sea!" Joe yelled.

Mike blinked against the salt water. He got down on his knees again. And again he tried to pry off the lid of the can.

Joe's voice echoed through the wind. "All right, damn it! You asked for it! Listen! It's cocaine! It's cocaine! You want me to spell it for you, Mike? C-O-C-A-I. . . ."

Mike felt something like shock, then a sort of sickness. He knew Tiger Joe smoked marijuana from time to time, and Mike didn't really care.

Mike wasn't involved with drugs himself, even though he knew some kids who were. But this was different. This had to do with another kind of involvement altogether. Mike said, "What do you do, buy it? Sell it?"

"I'm into this scene deep! You get the picture?"

"You sell it, right?" said Mike. "That's where you get your money, right? That's how come you never work!"

"You got it!" Tiger Joe yelled. "I'm a dealer! I'm like a middleman! But I never sell to kids like you—nothing like that. It's bigger, Mike—I deal with the big guys! You understand now?"

"I never. . . ." Mike didn't know what to say. He was stunned, but he was also angry. "How long have you been doing this? I mean, ever since I've known you? *How long, Joe? When?*"

Mike was standing up again, about six feet from the helm. Joe said, "I'm going to tell you. You know it now anyway. See, your old pal Tiger Joe isn't the nice guy you thought he was. I've been making this scene for years. Before I put in to Galway Bay. I mean, how do you think I got this gimpy leg? I got shot in the leg, man. I got shot. Even *that* didn't stop me. See how it is?"

"I don't believe you!"

"You'd *better* believe," Joe said. "There's no use kidding you now! That's the way it is!"

Joe was right—Mike had to believe him. Because it was all too clear now. Clear and very wrong. Mike hated everything that was happening.

Joe was saying, "Listen, Mike, I'm going to tell you something! The stuff comes up from Colombia every week or so! This is the biggest haul I ever handled, too. Mike . . . Mike, listen. If you stay cool, if you just get hold of yourself—if you just use your head—you can get out of this! You don't have to be part of this! I never wanted you to be part of it!"

"How?" Mike said. And now he felt filled with something very close to grief. He felt betrayed, too. There was something about this—about Joe's smuggling dope—that went beyond a lot of the things Mike already knew. And he felt as if, all along, Joe had been a fake and a phony, not a friend at all.

The waves were beginning to tower. They rose like silver-green mountains topped with froth, hovered, then folded and crashed down. The rain was like a solid curtain. Again lightning flashed.

Tiger Joe was having trouble keeping his footing. He called, "Mike! Mike! Take the wheel again! I've got to use the radio! Hurry up!"

Mike stumbled up. He fell again. Everything seemed to be happening at once. Crawling, he tried to reach the helm. Tiger Joe was thrown sideways. Another wave hovered and crashed on the deck.

Joe was muttering, "The radio . . . got to get help. Got to. Damn it, we're going under. . . . We . . . take this . . . Mike! Mike! Take it . . . *take it!*"

The life preserver. Tiger Joe had seized it. He threw it. He threw it over to Mike. And Mike caught it. Joe had thrown him the only life preserver on board. Mike shouted, "What are you. . . ."

Tiger Joe hurtled backward toward the rail. He cried out.

Darkness. Blackness. A wave so high, its trough so deep, that its coldness seemed to swallow Mike. It was as if he were being devoured. He was lifted up. Water caught and tossed him. It was a force greater than any force on land. Then, as he tried to hang on to the rail, Mike felt himself being seized, lifted, hurled.

He was falling through water. He flailed with his arms. He was overboard, and the boat had tilted crazily onto its side. The boat, the waves, the rain— they all seemed like one terrible thing in an eerie flash of lightning.

"Joe!" Mike tried to cry. But his mouth was filled with water, and he was alone in the thrashing sea. He knew he was going to die.

Moving through icy depths, gasping, the water in his mouth nearly drowning him, he struggled.

"Who. . . ."

". . . be all right. . . ."

"Kid. . . . Got any ID on him!"

"Conscious?"

"Head back toward Calusa Point. Still pretty rough around Galway Bay."

Mike opened his eyes. Where was he? On a boat of some kind. Men were around him. Men in uniform. He tried to speak.

"He's coming to," someone said.

"Where. . . ."

A man was standing over him.

"This is a Coast Guard cutter," the man said. "You're all right now."

"But how . . ." Mike began. "Where's Joe?"

"Who?"

"Tiger Joe."

"How many were on that boat?"

"Just me and Tiger Joe!"

The man shook his head. "We found you hanging on to that life preserver. You were about half conscious."

"But there's another guy!"

"We had a report—small craft in the area. We were out there a half hour or so. . . . There was nobody but you. . . . Your boat went under. . . ."

Suddenly everything ran back through Mike's mind all at once. It was like a film being run through a projector very fast. He saw Joe and the drugs and the towering waves and the life preserver. "You've got to go back!"

The man frowned. Then he signaled to one of the other men. "O.K., we'll give it another try. Can't stay out there long, though. Look at it this way, kid—you're lucky to be alive."

The Coast Guard vessel stayed at sea for another hour without finding a sign of Tiger Joe. Finally, despite Mike's pleas, the men in uniform gave up and headed back toward land. It was afternoon when they put in to shore. The sky was still dark, and rain still poured down.

They were at the Coast Guard station a few miles south of town. The coastguardsmen took Mike into a brightly lighted, warm room. One man went into another room and came back with some dry dungarees. Mike put them on. Another man phoned Mike's parents and told them that Mike was all right.

Mike sat near a large desk and told the men what he could remember about the storm. He said that he and Tiger Joe had just gone out for a cruise—that they hadn't expected such bad weather. He mentioned seeing another small boat—the trawler. But he didn't say anything about drugs. He didn't know what good that would do now.

One of the coastguardsmen wrote down what Mike said. After about a half hour, they told him they had enough information. One of the men took

Mike out to an official car. They set out through the rain.

Fifteen minutes later they pulled up in front of Mike's house.

"Michael!" Alice Denton ran from the front door through the rain. She hugged Mike as he got out of the car. The coastguardsman waved and drove off. Lou Denton was waiting at the door. He embraced his son. But Mike didn't know if his father was still angry with him or not.

A few minutes later, as they sat in the living room, Lou Denton said, "Thank God you're safe. But what were you doing out there, Mike? Why? When we woke up this morning, you were gone. Why?"

"I. . . ." Mike didn't know how to begin. Too many things had happened now. And besides, something inside his head seemed to be spinning. Spinning like a gray-green whirlpool.

"Something's the matter." It was his father's voice.

"Don't you feel well, Michael?" asked his mother gently.

"I'm sick, I think," said Mike. "I . . . I really feel awful."

"We'd better get him to bed," Lou Denton said.

Then it was as if the sea were closing over him again. He could feel his parents leading him, practically carrying him to his room. He felt hot and cold at the same time. Somebody was taking off his clothes.

He floated. He seemed to float for a long time. He floated through all the years of his childhood and all the days of the year. He floated into the future, into a time when he was as old as Tiger Joe and traveled to distant lands, and till he was as old as his parents and older than Mr. Crane. He floated through oceans and rivers and worlds he had never seen.

"Mike . . . Michael?"

Pale light seemed to filter through his eyelids.

"It's afternoon, Michael."

He opened his eyes. His mother was standing by his bed, holding a tray.

"Afternoon?"

"You've slept nearly twenty-four hours. You were delirious. The doctor was here."

"What's that?" He pointed to the tray.

"I fixed you some eggs." She put the tray on a table beside his bed.

Slowly, Mike ate the food his mother had prepared. It tasted good, and he realized he was very hungry—famished.

When he had finished, his mother sat in a chair near his bed and said, "Michael, while you were asleep—sick—we got a phone call. It was those Coast Guard men again. They found . . . they found the boat. . . . I mean, pieces of it . . . the *Tiger Lily*. . . ."

"Pieces of the *Tiger Lily*?" Mike pushed himself up in bed. "Joe . . . what about Joe?"

Mrs. Denton shook her head. "They don't know," she said. "They haven't any sign of him."

The storm—that was more than twenty-four hours ago, and Joe still had not been found. Mike felt very worried. The cocaine—that didn't seem to matter much now, if only Joe was safe. And with a kind of forced optimism, Mike tried to figure out what had happened. They had been at least ten miles out when the storm came up. Could Joe have swum—clung to something? Another boat! Maybe Joe had been picked up by another boat! Yes, Mike thought. Maybe the trawler that had made contact with the *Tiger Lily*—maybe that trawler had come along and picked Joe up. . . .

"Can I get you anything else, Mike?" his mother asked.

Mike shook his head. Suddenly, his eyes began to hurt. They still seemed to sting from the sea water.

He turned away from his mother, closed his eyes, and put his face against the pillow.

The rest of that day Mike stayed in bed. Much of the time he slept. But every time he woke up he thought of Tiger Joe, and how Joe had thrown him the life preserver. That night, Mike slept a long time. The next morning he got up and got dressed. The doctor had said he didn't have to go to school the rest of this week. Mike didn't care at all. Because there was so much on his mind.

For one thing, the trouble with Mr. Crane was still hanging over his head. His father had referred to the matter only once since the storm. He had said, "Mike, I know how hard all this is. But when you're better, don't forget what I said. *Somebody's going to have to do something about that fire. And you know what you should do.*"

When Mike woke up the next morning, he made up his mind. He felt wretched about everything. And he feared for Tiger Joe's safety. But he knew now that—even though he hated the idea—he would have to do what his father asked. He realized now that it was the best thing to do, after all. He didn't spend much time at breakfast. When he had finished eating, he got up and headed for the door. When his mother asked where he was going, he just said, "I'll be back in a little while."

"Be careful. Remember how sick you've been," said Mrs. Denton.

"Yeah, but I feel a lot better," said Mike. "I'm fine now."

Mike wasn't really fine. He felt weak, and a little shaky. But this came first.

He started walking toward Palm Drive. It was a small street at the other end of town, and he knew Mr. Crane lived there. As Mike walked, he thought about what he was going to say, and how he was going to say it. But the words kept getting tangled in his mind.

Mr. Crane's house was a small bungalow. There were two tall palm trees outside on the lawn.

As Mike approached the house, he hesitated. For an instant, he seemed to hear echoes of the storm again.

Then he walked up to Mr. Crane's front door and rang the bell.

Nothing happened.

He waited. He rang again.

Finally the door opened part way, and Mike could see Mr. Crane standing there. At Mr. Crane's feet was a black-and-white cat. The cat peered up at Mike.

Mr. Crane was frowning. He was a thin man, with hollow cheeks. He wore horn-rimmed glasses, and as his eyes met Mike's, they seemed to harden behind their thick lenses. He said, "Mike Denton— isn't it?"

Mike said, "I guess . . . I guess you're surprised to see me, Mr. Crane."

"I am," the man said. "I'm very surprised."

"Mr. Crane, could I . . . could I come in and talk to you?" Mike could feel his heart pounding. "It's important. I. . . ."

"What do you want to talk to me about?" said

Mr. Crane. His voice was high-pitched and strained.

"About . . . about everything," said Mike.

"Well. . . ." Mr. Crane seemed undecided. He looked past Mike, toward the street. Finally he said, "I'm busy. . . . I don't have much time."

"It's important, Mr. Crane. Really important."

Mr. Crane frowned again.

"Please, Mr. Crane," said Mike.

Mr. Crane tapped his fingers nervously against the door. At last he said, "Well . . . you can come in for a minute. But that's all."

Mike stepped inside. The cat turned and fled, its claws scratching on the bare floor. Mike followed Mr. Crane down a hall into the living room. The room was sparsely furnished and neat. On a table near a window was a model sailing ship. It was a lot like the one Mike and Gary had burned.

Mr. Crane pointed toward the sofa, and Mike sat down. Mr. Crane perched on the edge of a chair.

Finally Mike got up enough courage to speak.

He could hear his own voice crack as he said, "Mr. Crane . . . Listen . . . I wanted to talk to you, because. . . . I mean, I heard how you want to press charges against me and all. I mean, going to the D.A. and everything. But you know, the other day—the fire—I mean, it just started as a joke. . . ."

Mr. Crane shook his head. His expression was twisted. He said, "I don't know what to make of your generation. You admit this . . . this crime, and now you come here expecting me to be sympathetic. Don't you know how much damage you caused?"

"A lot," said Mike. "I guess it was pretty bad."

"It's a disgrace! I knew that you were one of the boys who had set the fire. I knew that from the start. It was my intention to seek a legal remedy. There's a lot of money involved, too. Do you realize that? Do you have any idea how much it's going to take to repair the building? To say nothing of my ship. . . ." He glared at Mike as he said, "I spent nearly a year working on that ship. It was a scale model of a Spanish galleon. . . ."

Mike felt as if he were sweating. He said, "I thought that maybe I could make it up to you, Mr. Crane. I don't have much money. But maybe we can figure out some way. Can't we talk about it?"

Mr. Crane stood up. "I don't think talking about it is going to do any good. The damage has been done."

Mike's breath seemed to flutter inside him. He said, "All I'm asking is . . . Mr. Crane, I'm not perfect . . . I made a big mistake . . . Mr. Crane, I'm only sixteen . . . I want a chance. . . ."

"People have to make their own chances in life," said Mr. Crane, starting toward the door. "You're old enough to know that. And I have work to do."

Leaving Mr. Crane's house, Mike felt sure that their conversation had just made things worse. Mr. Crane was a bitter man, and he obviously didn't like Mike, or probably most other kids Mike's age. And if Mr. Crane brought the law down on Mike, how could Mike handle things? And if Mike got a criminal record, what would become of him?

And then there was still Tiger Joe. With every hour that passed, Mike grew more worried. Surely, Mike thought, if Joe was all right, they would have heard something by now.

Slowly, Mike walked back toward the center of town. At least he had done what his father had asked—he had talked to Mr. Crane.

When Mike got home, his mother met him at the door. Her face looked drawn. She said, "Come in and sit down, Michael. I want to talk to you."

"What about?"

Alice Denton gestured toward the kitchen. He followed her. She sat down at the kitchen table, and he took a chair across from her.

"Michael," she said. "Mike . . . your friend . . . Joe. . . ."

"Tiger Joe?"

She seemed flustered.

"What about Joe?" Mike asked.

"There was a . . . a phone call," she said.

"When?"

"While you were gone."

"Just now?"

"Yes. It was those men at the Coast Guard station. They asked for you. I told them. . . ."

"Well?" said Mike.

His mother looked up and said, "Mike . . . your friend. . . . They found him." Her fingers were pressed against the table.

"They found . . . Joe. . . ."

"They found his body," she said.

"Tiger Joe. . . ."

"About fifteen miles south of town. Just this morning, they said. . . ."

Mike pushed his chair back. He got up and left the kitchen. As he walked to his room, he saw the storm again, in his mind. He heard the wind, and he heard Tiger Joe's voice calling out. Mike had never felt so alone in his life.

That afternoon, Gary came over. He and Mike sat in Mike's room and talked. They talked about Tiger Joe and how they felt. And Mike told Gary how, if it hadn't been for Joe, Mike might have drowned. And how Joe may have given his own life in order to save Mike's.

For a long time they talked about Tiger Joe, about some of the good times they had had. They talked about what a strange guy Joe had been, how hard to figure out. Then they were quiet.

Suddenly, Gary said, "Listen. I've been thinking this thing over. Old man Crane is really going to push it all the way—right?"

Mike nodded. "I wouldn't be surprised."

Gary shook his head. "It's all wrong," he said. "You know as well as I do—*I* set that fire."

"That's not the point," Mike said. "I was with you. I was in on it."

"No, this is important," said Gary. "I've been thinking. . . . I ought to admit what I did."

They continued to talk. They argued about it. Finally, Mike got Gary to promise not to say anything. At least not yet. Then they talked for another half hour— mostly about Tiger Joe. It was close to dinnertime when Gary left.

Mike sat looking out the window. He found himself thinking about Joe on shore, Joe on the boat, Joe telling stories about other cities, other countries, people he had met. Then all the images seemed to blur, and he seemed to see Joe at the helm again, in the storm, reaching for the life preserver. And Mike wondered: How many people would give up a boat's only life preserver to save another person's life?

That night at dinner, Mike talked to his parents again—about the storm, about Tiger Joe, about the fire. He told them how he had gone to see Mr. Crane, and how it hadn't done any good.

Lou Denton said, "At least you went to see him. That's something."

"But it didn't work, Dad. He wouldn't listen."

"Still, it was the right thing to do."

At about eight o'clock, while they were in the living room, the door bell rang.

Lou Denton got up and went to the door. When he came back, Mr. Crane was with him.

Mike was astonished. And at first, Mr. Crane seemed to avoid looking at Mike.

Alice Denton smiled nervously. Then she asked Mr. Crane to come into the living room. They all went into the living room and sat down. At first everyone seemed stiff. But as they sat and talked, Mike began to realize something: Mr. Crane's attitude seemed to have changed.

"I. . . ." Mr. Crane began. Then glancing at Lou and Alice Denton he said, "This is a bit difficult for me. A bit difficult to. . . . Well, you see, the way we spoke this morning. . . . When your son came to see me this morning, I'm afraid I wasn't exactly in the mood for conversation. And maybe I—maybe I could have handled things a bit differently." He turned toward Mike and cleared his throat, saying, "You were with this man, this Joe Easton, in the storm. . . ."

"On the *Tiger Lily*," Mike said. "Yes. . . ."

"And you were rescued, while he. . . ."

"Tiger Joe was at the wheel," Mike said. "He threw me the life preserver. He must have known what would happen. . . ."

Mr. Crane drew himself up in his chair. He looked very uncomfortable. He said, "I heard about Joe Easton's death this afternoon. You know, the truth is . . . I never liked the man. I didn't think he was a good sort—the sort we want down at the marina." He paused and looked down at his hands. "But I'll admit that I can be wrong. And I realize that . . . that you, Mike . . . I realize that you had a lot to say to me this morning. And I refused to listen."

"Yes, but—" Mike began.

"And then, today, when I heard that Easton had died, it hit me all of a sudden," Mr. Crane went on. "It hit me . . . how silly some of our differences really are. The man is dead, and I'm still worrying about a model ship. You know, Michael, it dawned on me that it took some courage for you to come talk to me this morning. I should have been a better host."

"Mr. Crane, you were a good enough host," Mike said. "It's just that—"

Mr. Crane turned to Lou Denton and said, "I've come here so we can settle this thing. Your son seems to have a head on his shoulders. And I certainly don't want to see his life ruined because of one mistake. Besides, it seems to me Michael has been through about enough these past few days. Can we get down to business?"

After that, they talked for a long time. Mike made some suggestions, and Mr. Crane made some suggestions, and Mr. and Mrs. Denton made suggestions, too. For almost another hour they continued to talk.

Finally they came to an understanding. Mr. Crane agreed not to press for a legal punishment.

Instead, they decided that Mike would work after school every afternoon, down at the marina. And he would work there next summer, too. But he would receive only half his pay. The other half of his pay would go to Mr. Crane—to the corporation that ran the marina, really—to pay for the damage the fire had caused.

When Mr. Crane was ready to go, he shook hands with Mike's parents. He shook Mike's hand, too. Then he looked from one of them to the other, as if there was something else he wanted to say. But he said nothing. He turned and left, and the door closed behind him.

They stood there in the hall—Mike and his parents. Mike said, "I don't really mind so much. I like it down at the marina. I won't mind working down there. That Crane—he's kind of weird, isn't he? But he was fair enough tonight. I have to admit that."

Later, as Mike headed for bed, he turned to glance at his chart in the hall. It was gone.

He knocked on his parents' bedroom door. When his father opened it, Mike said, "Dad, my chart. . . ."

"You don't need that thing anymore," Lou

Denton said. "I guess from now on, most things will have to be up to you. You know, *I've* made some mistakes, too." He put his hand gently on Mike's arm, saying, "Now go to bed, Son. Sleep well."

The next afternoon, Tiger Joe's brother arrived from Iowa. He was going to take Joe's body home on a plane.

Mike did not want to be with his friends now. He didn't want to be with anybody. He made a phone call and found out when the plane was going to leave. Alone, he walked to the small airfield at the edge of town. From a distance, he watched while four men loaded a simple coffin onto a plane. As he watched, Mike realized that Tiger Joe's body was inside that coffin—and he tried to visualize it. Tiger Joe—drowned. Mike didn't really want to visualize Tiger Joe now, but something in his mind forced him to. And for a minute or so it was difficult for him to look at the coffin. Then he looked at it hard. And he watched Tiger Joe's brother—a man in a business suit, a man Joe had not even liked very much—accompany the coffin to the plane.

Mike had never fully understood Tiger Joe. Because Joe seemed to be a combination of all sorts of people, all sorts of good and bad men, all rolled into one. But, Mike thought, did that make Joe so different from most people in the world? Wasn't everybody a combination of all kinds of things?

For a moment, Mike closed his eyes. He said a little prayer for Joe. Then he turned and began walking toward home. He wasn't at all sure about everything that had happened over the past few days. There were still far too many things for him to grasp. He thought about his parents. And then he thought about the other kids in school. Mike didn't know how much he would ever tell them about Joe and the drugs. Probably, he would never say a word to anyone. But he could decide that in the future. If there were rules in life, he thought, a lot of them were going to have to be his own rules now—things he had learned through his own experience. And when it came to Gary, well, if Gary wanted to speak out—to tell Mr. Crane that he was responsible for the fire—then let him. Maybe both of them would end up working down at the marina after school. That wouldn't be such a bad outcome after all.

Behind him, Mike could hear the plane starting down the runway. And he heard the high whine of the plane's engines as it took off.

But he didn't look back.

He reached into his pocket. His fingers touched the harmonica Joe had given him. He had almost forgotten it. He pulled it out and looked at it. He ran his fingers over its metal sides—smooth, silvery metal etched with fanciful designs. Tiger Joe had told him he had got the harmonica years ago from a street salesman in Yugoslavia. What was it the man had said? Something about how the harmonica would play all by itself. Something about how you had to have heart. But none of that made much sense to Mike.

But what if it was true? Or—in some fantastic way—true and false at the same time? Could that be possible? Is the truth about things in life—about yourself, about other people, about your family and your friends—really so easy to figure out?

The harmonica gleamed in the sun. One of these days, Mike knew, he would be able to play it, and play it well.